There's a
LION
in the Forest!

Mônica Carnesi

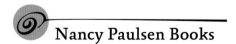

Nancy Paulsen Books

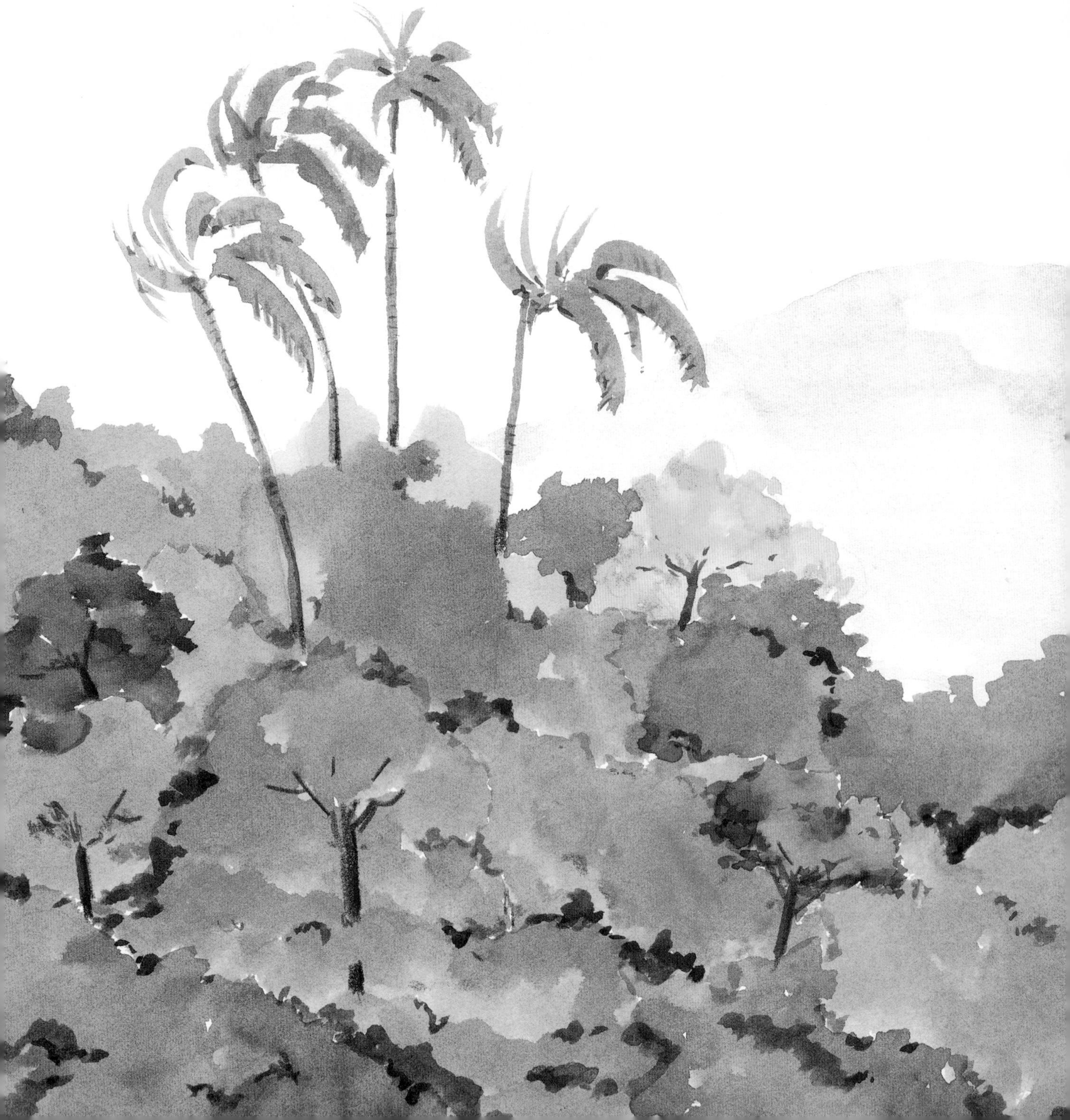

Deep in the Atlantic Forest of Brazil, a new sound traveled through the trees.

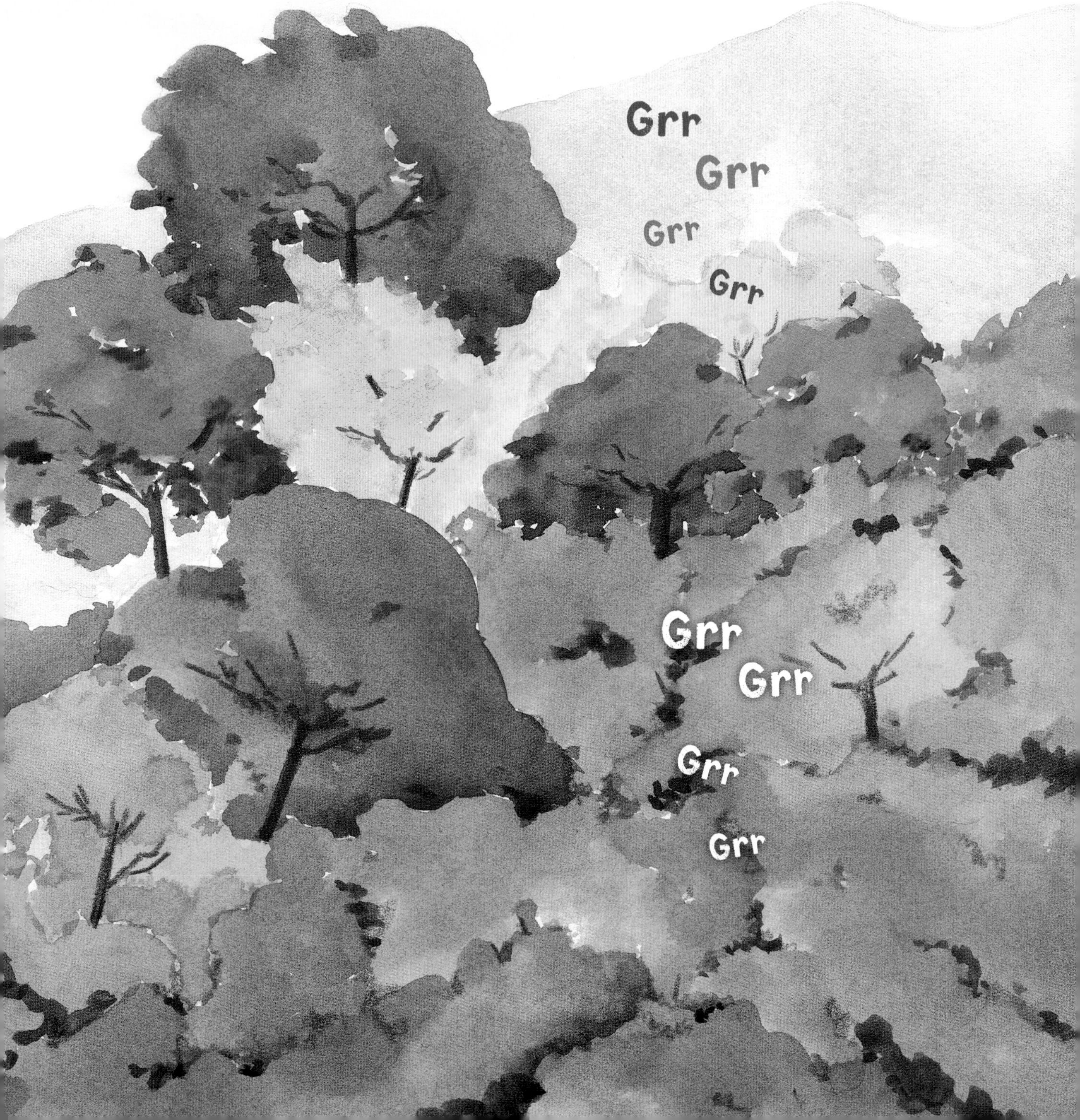
Grr
Grr
Grr
Grr
Grr
Grr
Grr
Grr

Toucan heard it first.

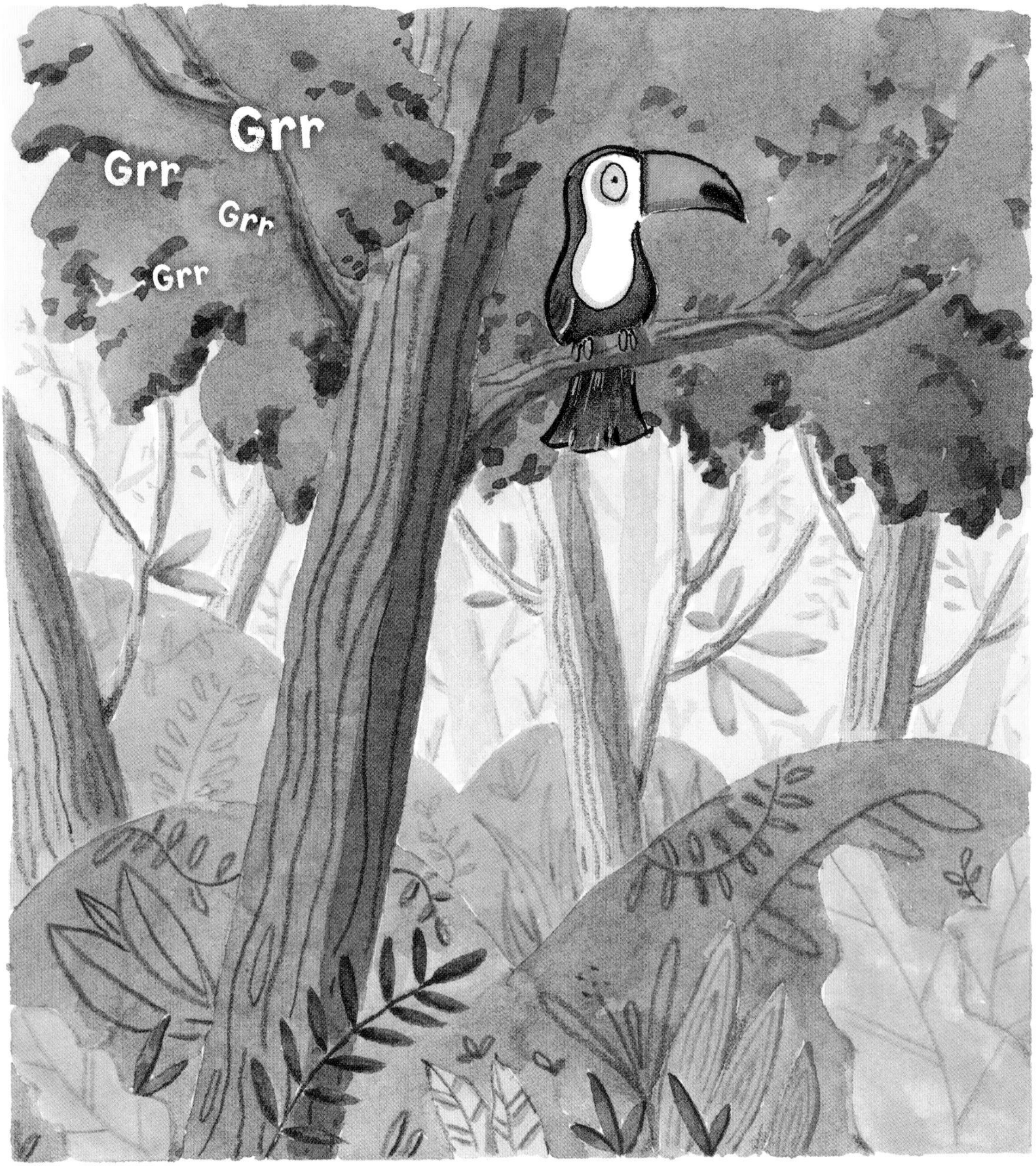
Grr
Grr
Grr
Grr

It was deep. It was growly.
It was a deep, growly growl.

That could only mean one thing.

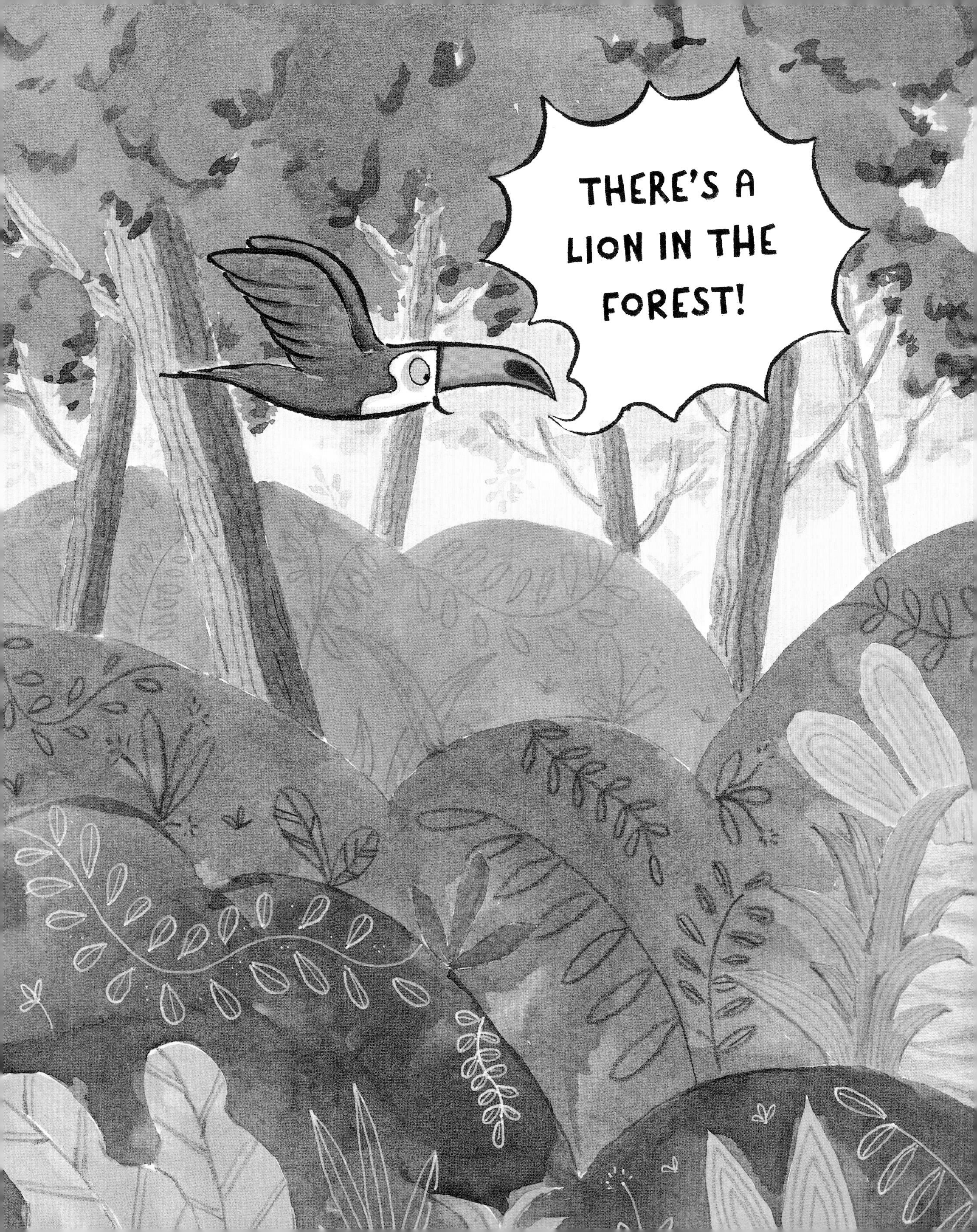
THERE'S A LION IN THE FOREST!

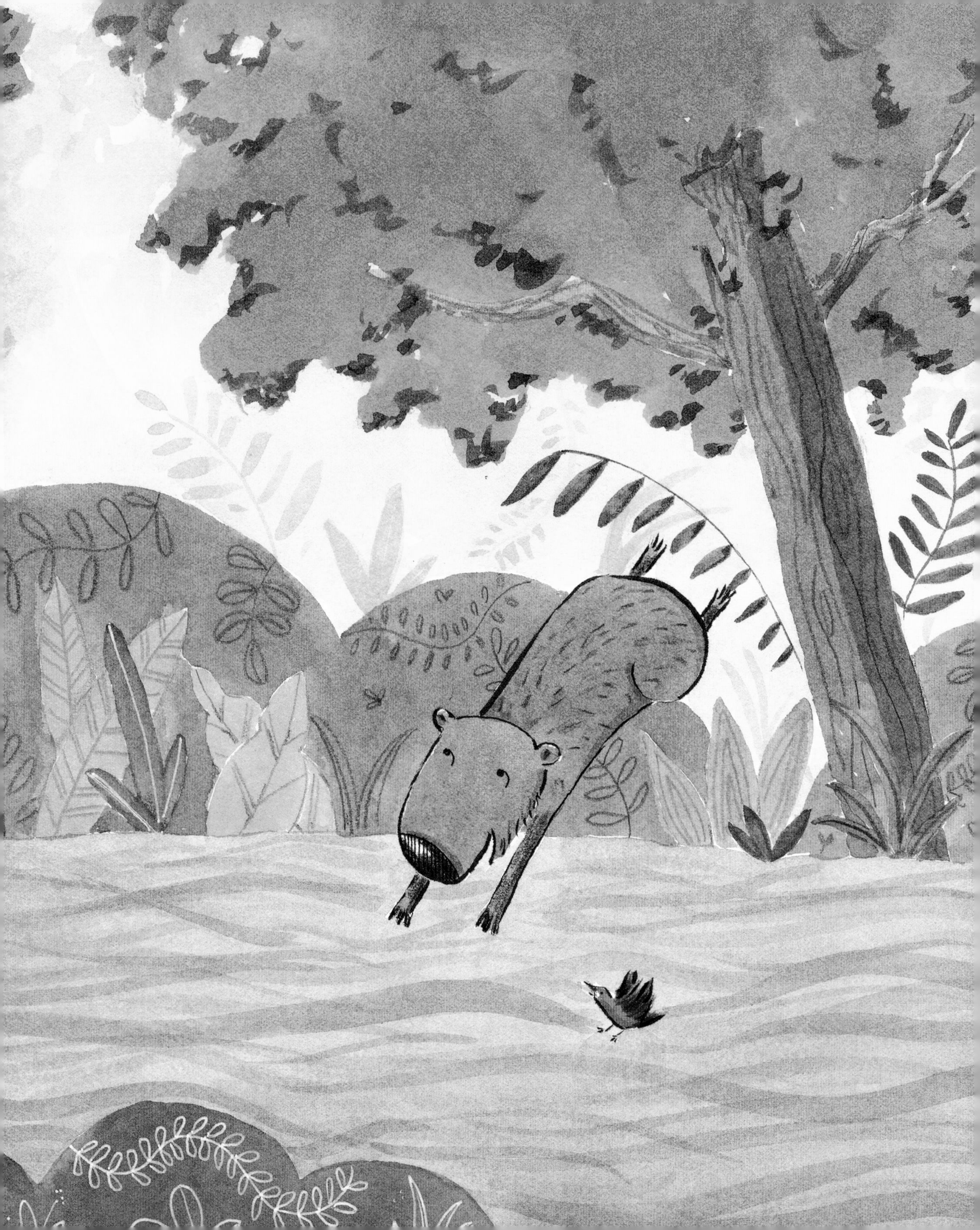

But Capybara was not alarmed.

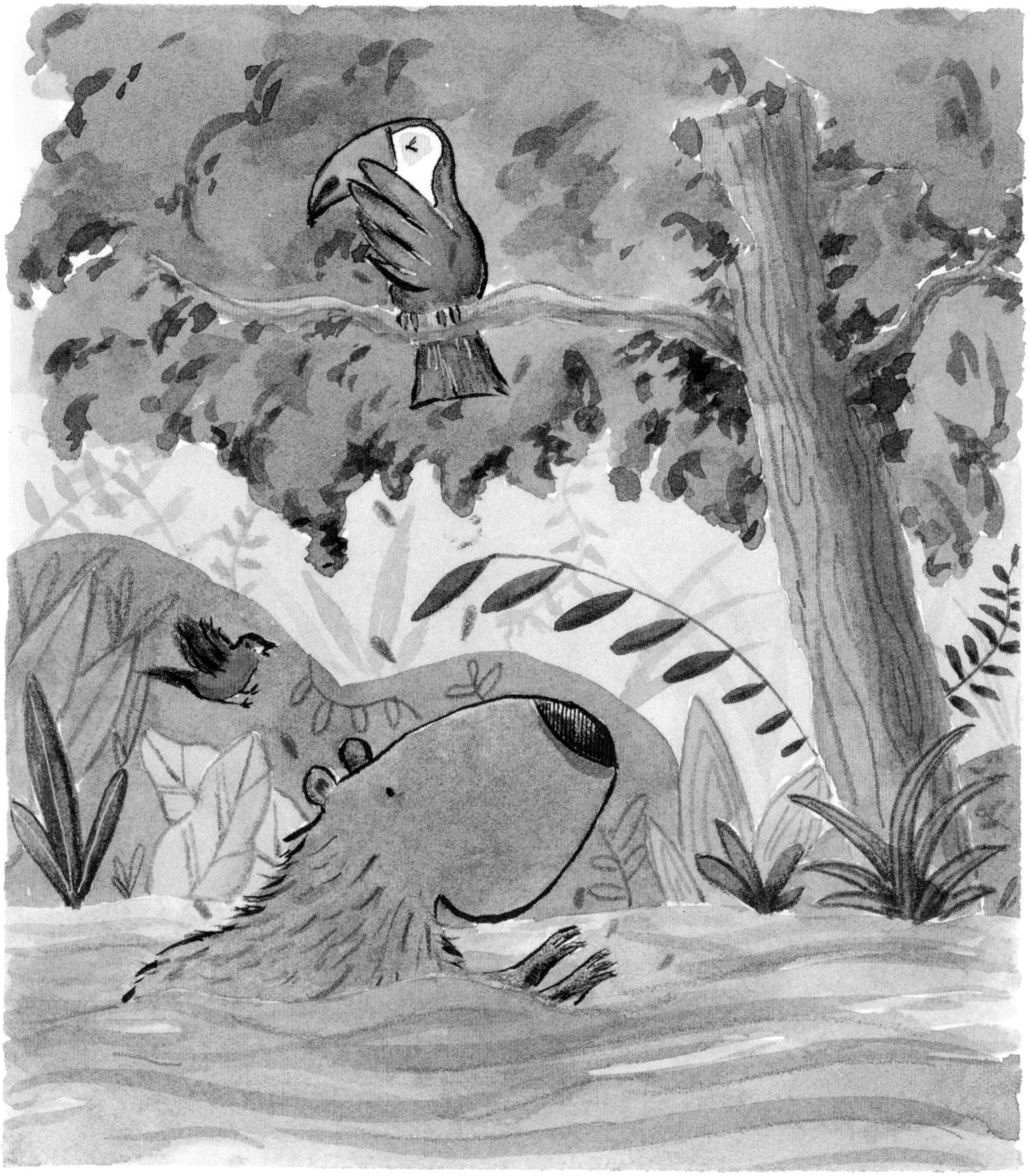

"We're in South America," she said.
"There are NO lions here."

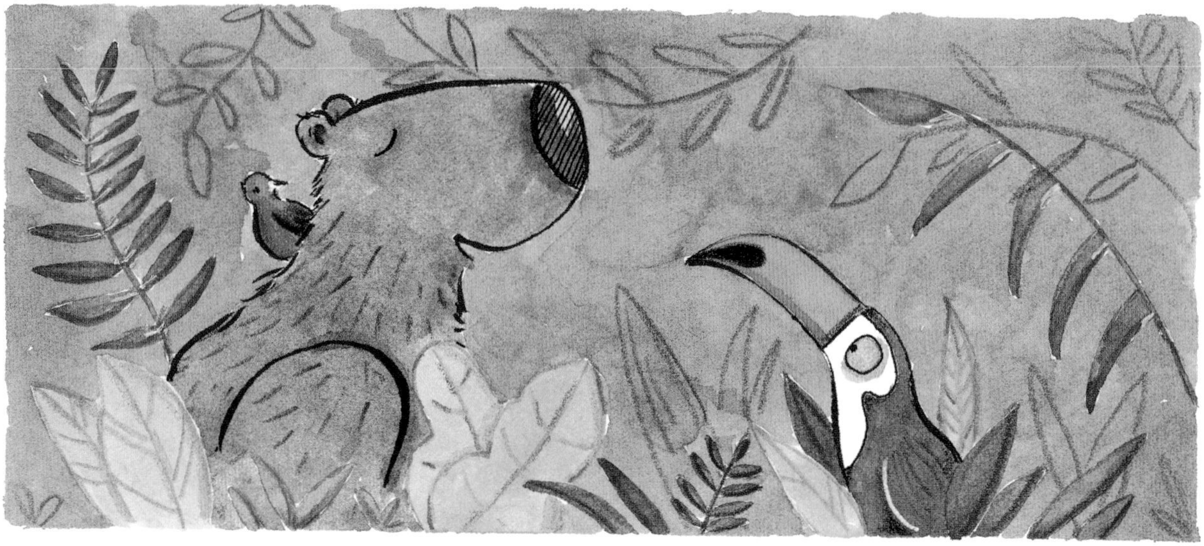

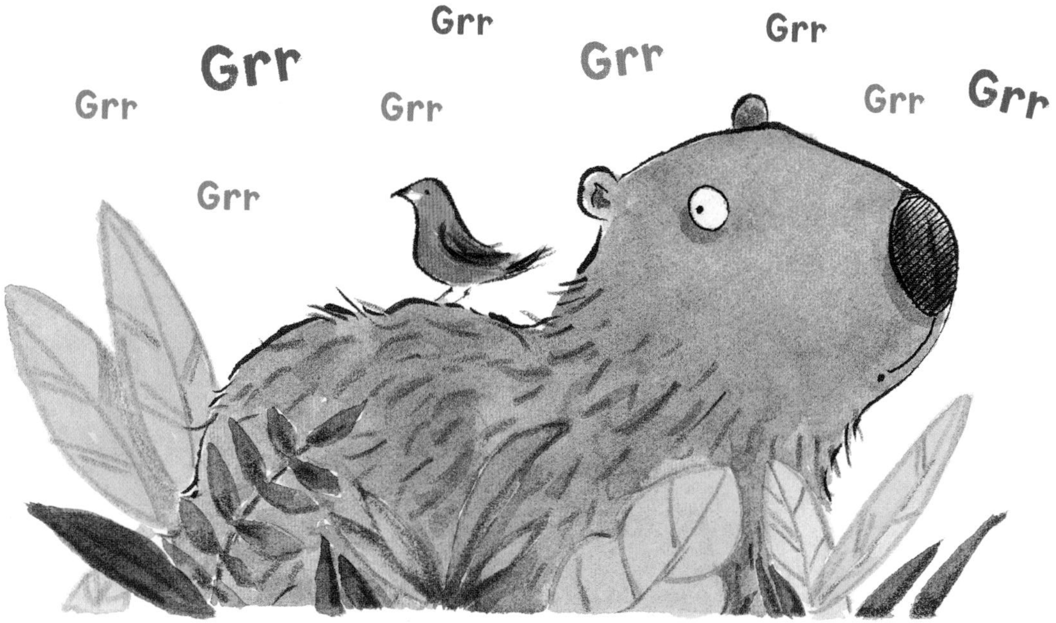
Grr
Grr
Grr
Grr
Grr
Grr
Grr
Grr
Grr

“Listen! It’s the growly growl again!” said Toucan.

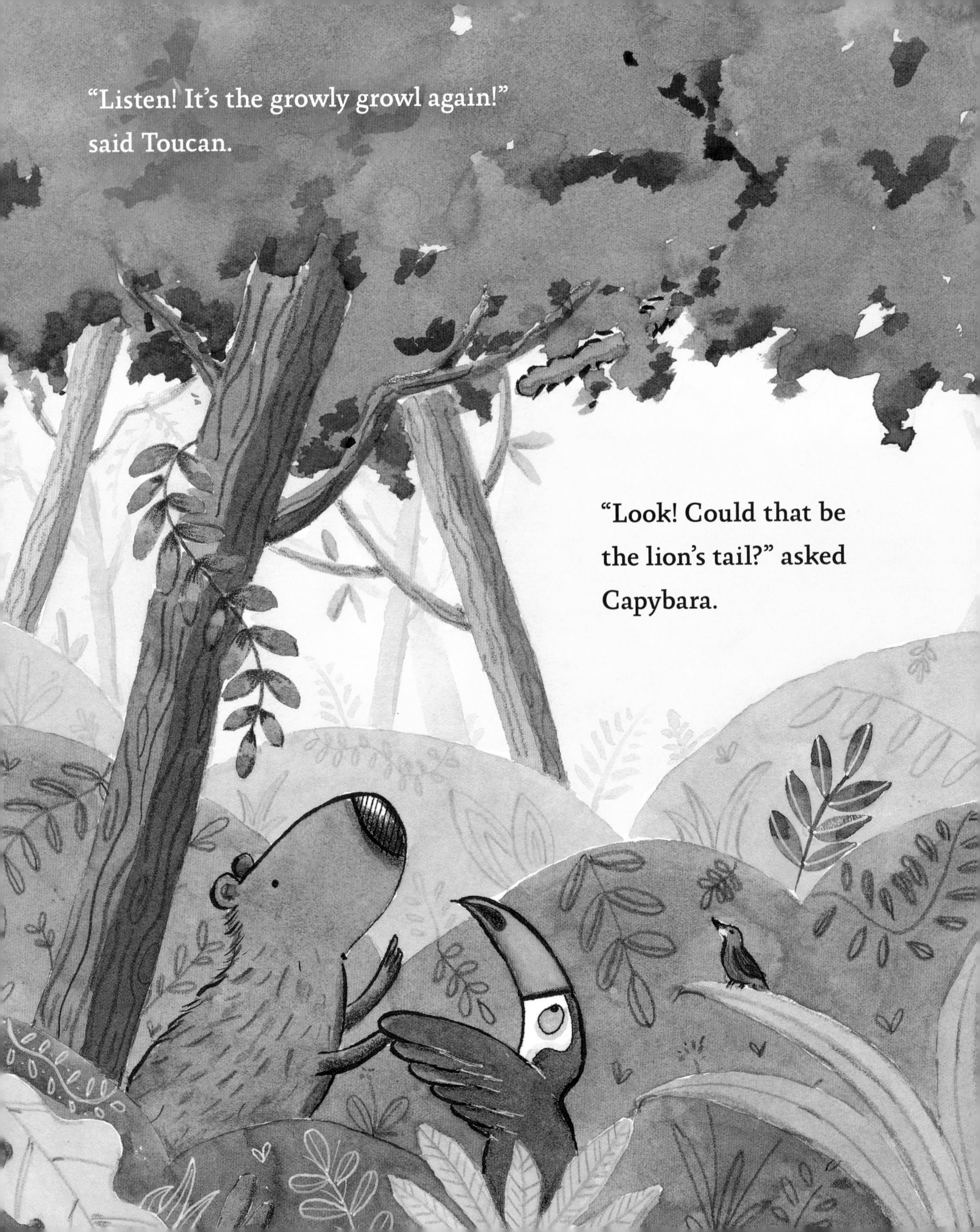

“Look! Could that be the lion’s tail?” asked Capybara.

It was long. It was terrifying.
It was a long, terrifying tail!

That could only mean one thing.

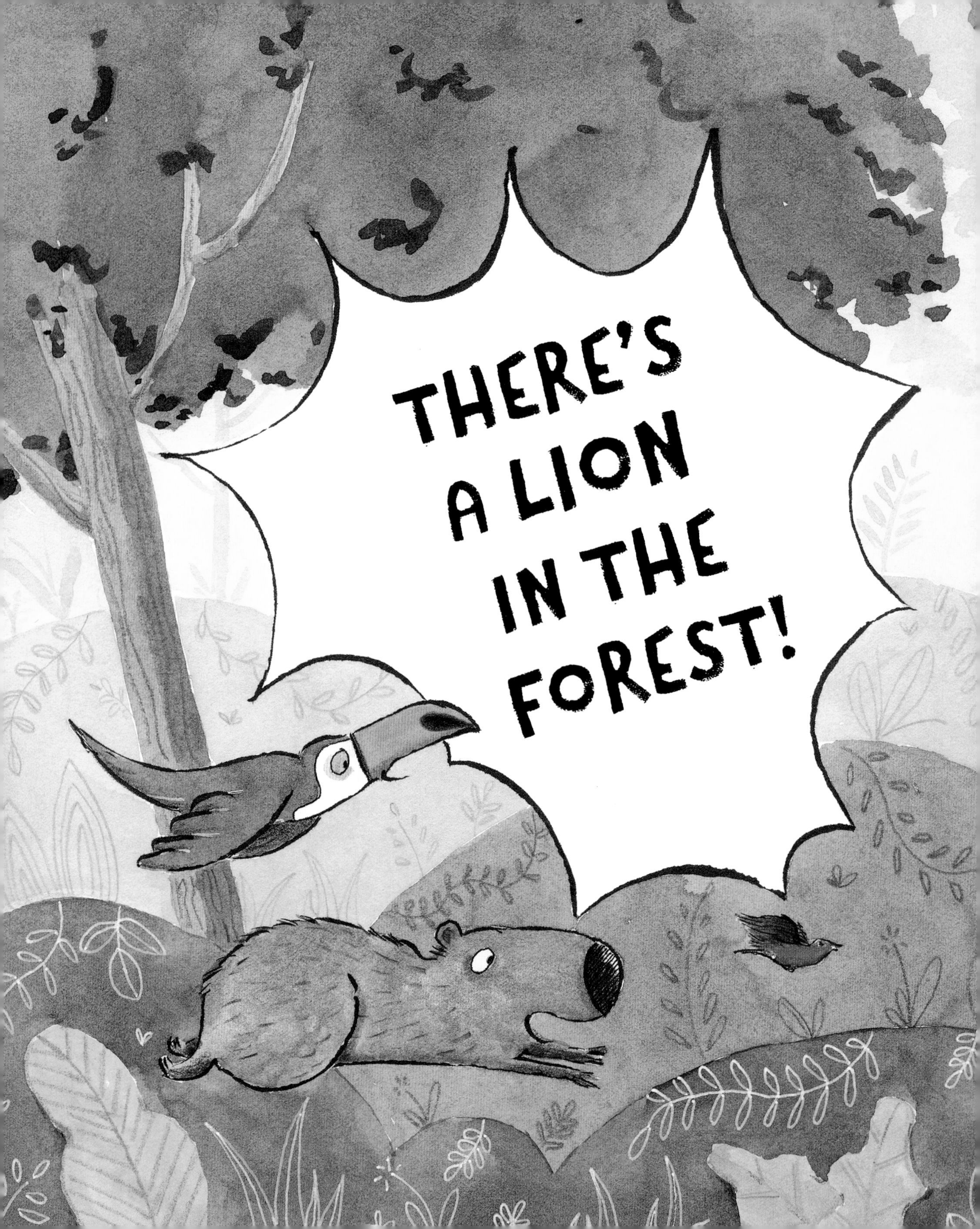
THERE'S A LION IN THE FOREST!

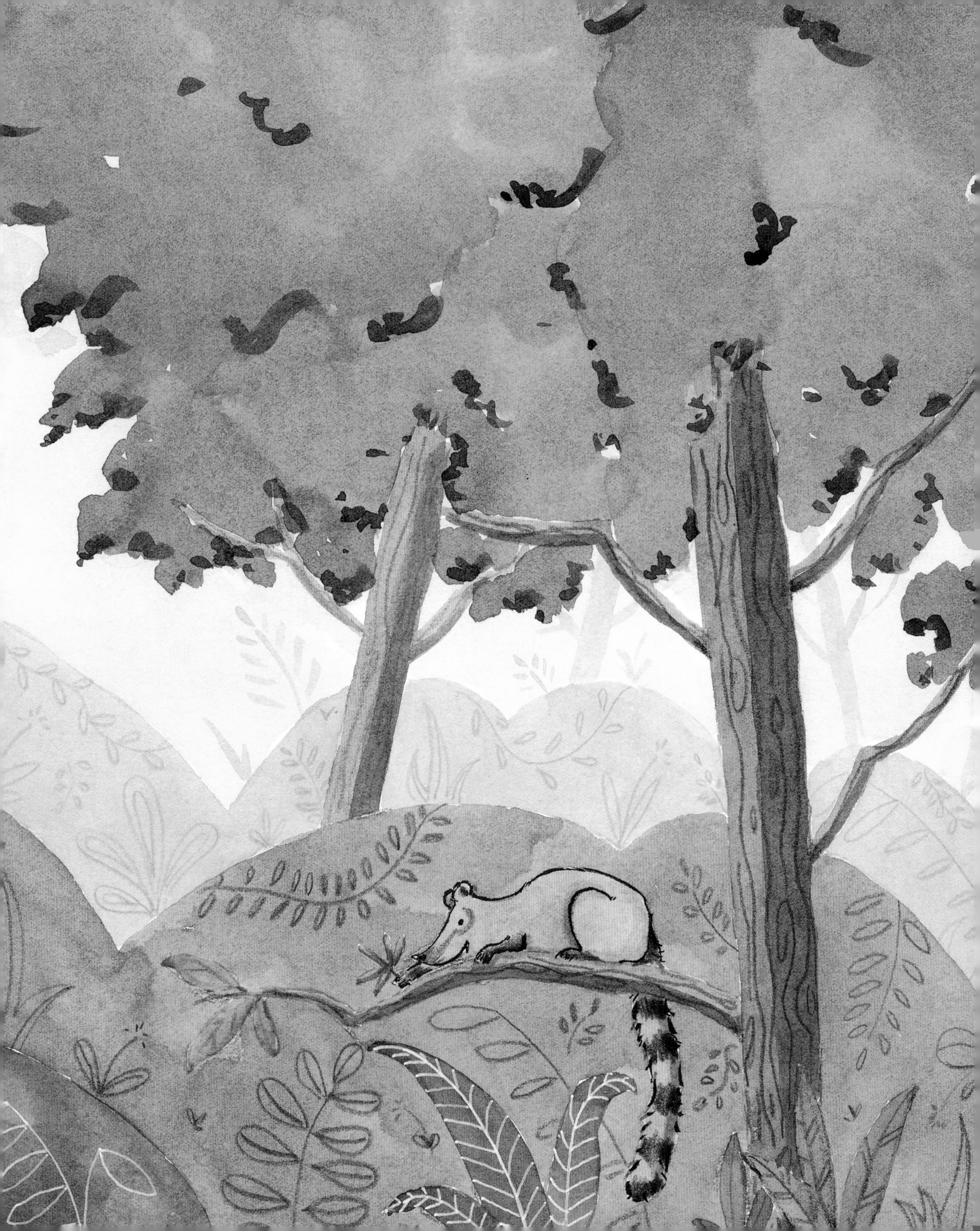

Coati was very confused.

"Did you say *lion*?" he asked. "But that's impossible. Lions live in savannas, and this is a tropical forest."

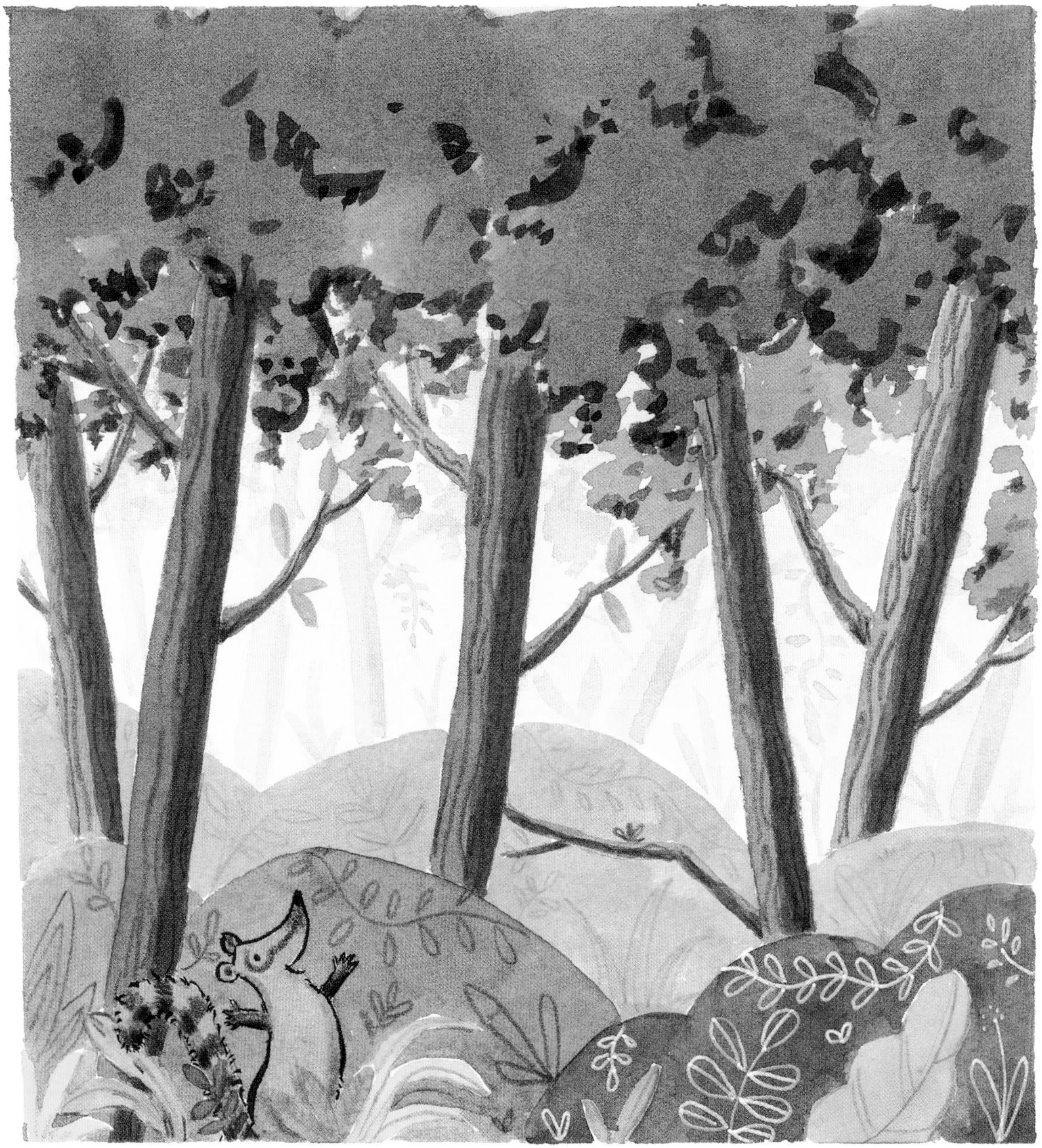

"That's what I thought, too," said Capybara.

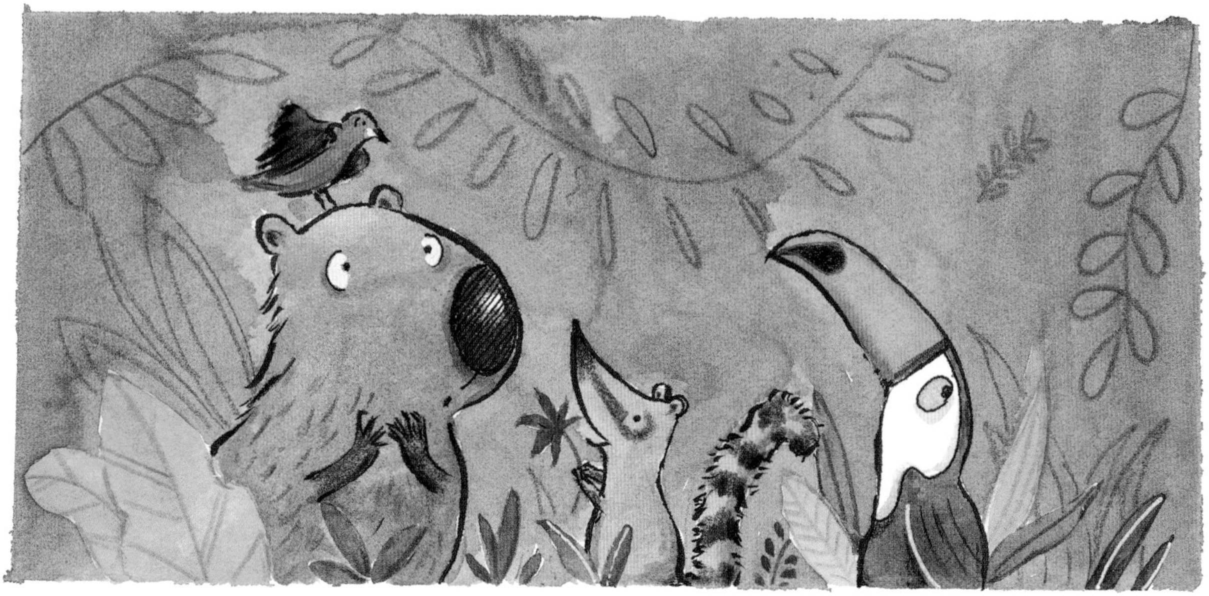

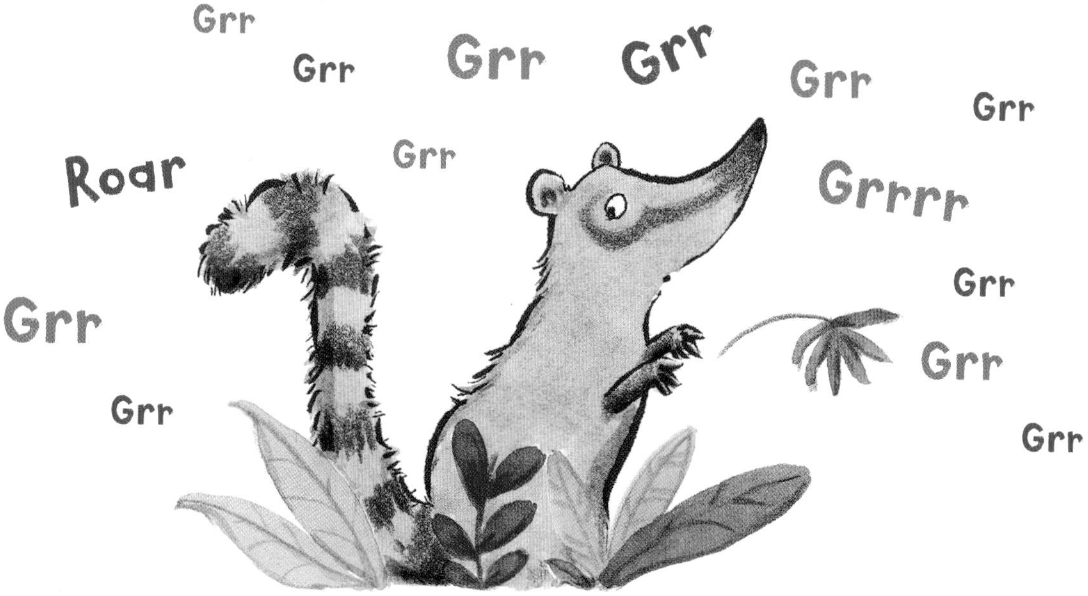
Grr
Grr
Grr
Grr
Grr
Grr
Roar
Grr
Grrrr
Grr
Grr
Grr
Grr
Grr

"Oh no! It's the growly growl again," wailed Toucan.

"And the terrifying tail!" cried Capybara.

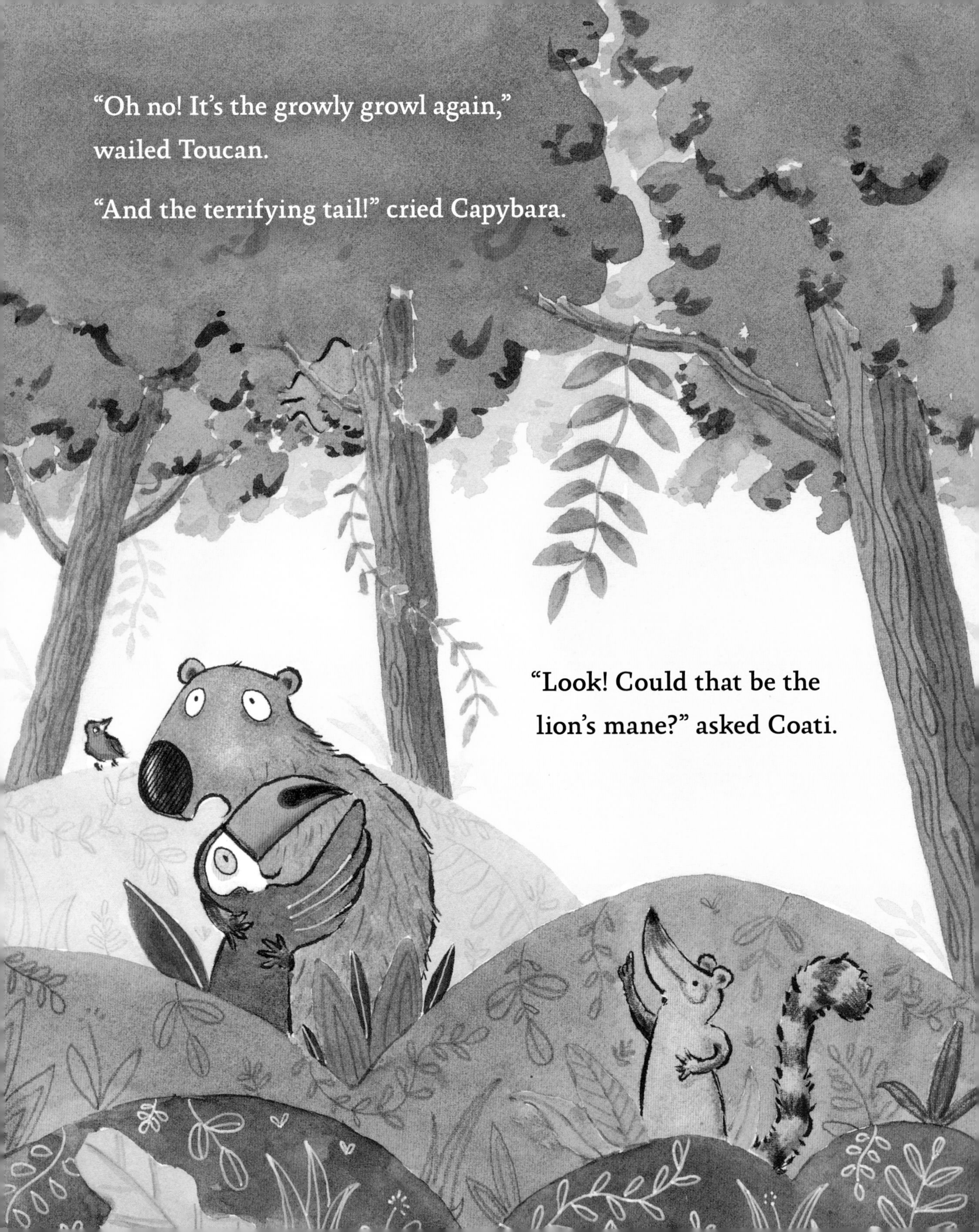

"Look! Could that be the lion's mane?" asked Coati.

It was thick. It was menacing.
It was a thick, menacing mane.

That could only
mean one thing.

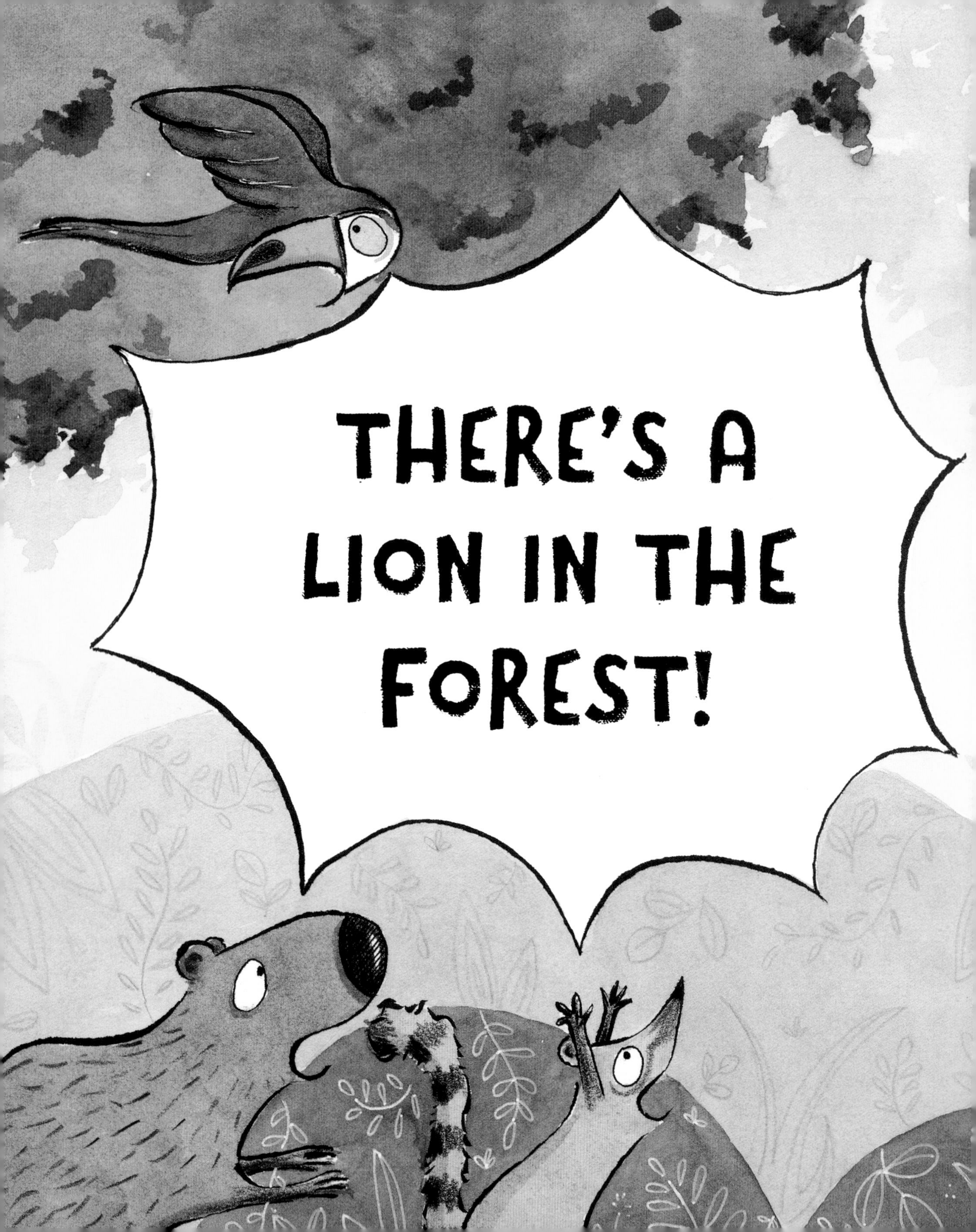
THERE'S A LION IN THE FOREST!

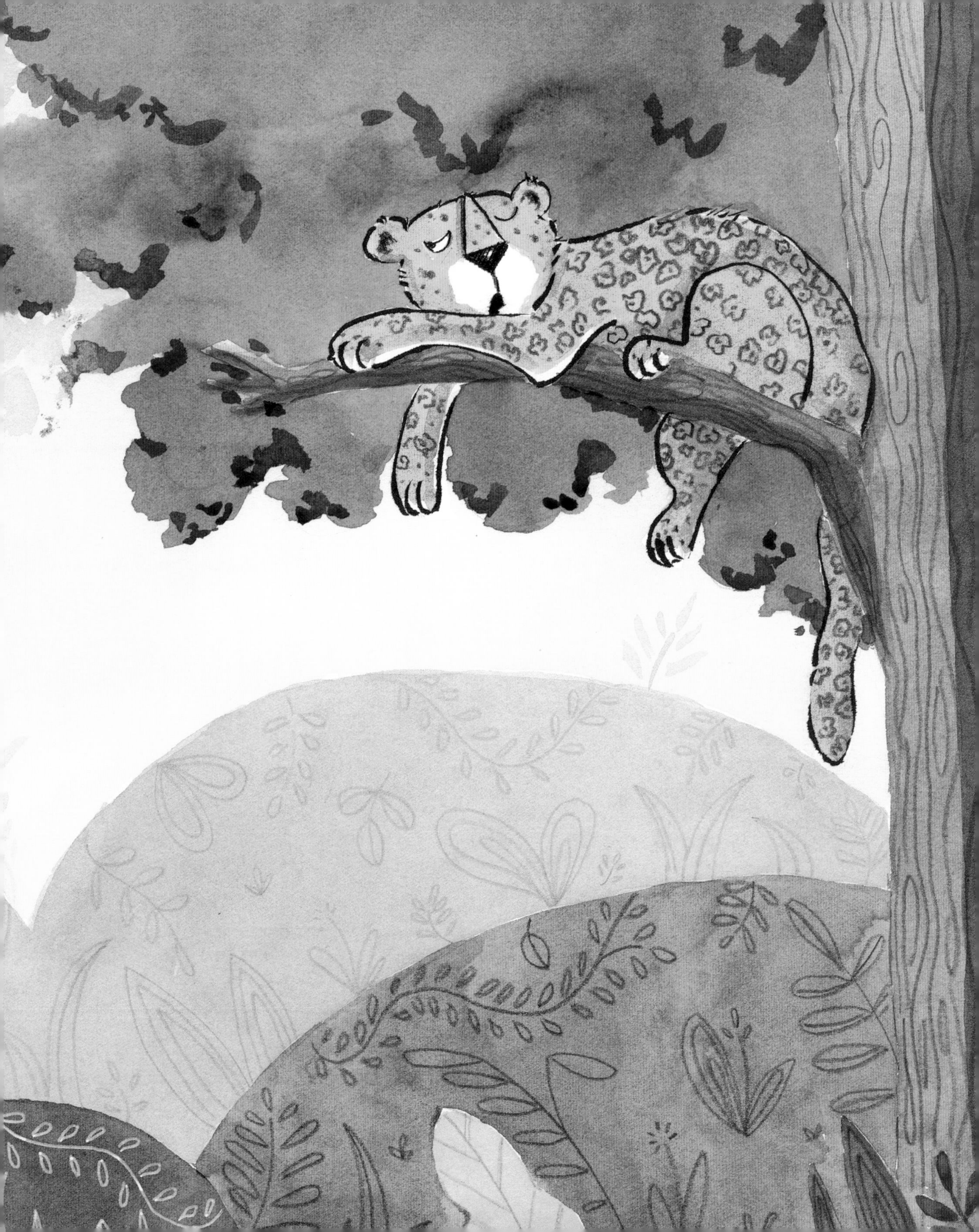

But Jaguar was remarkably calm.

“What’s all this talk about a lion?” he said. “There are no lions in South America.”

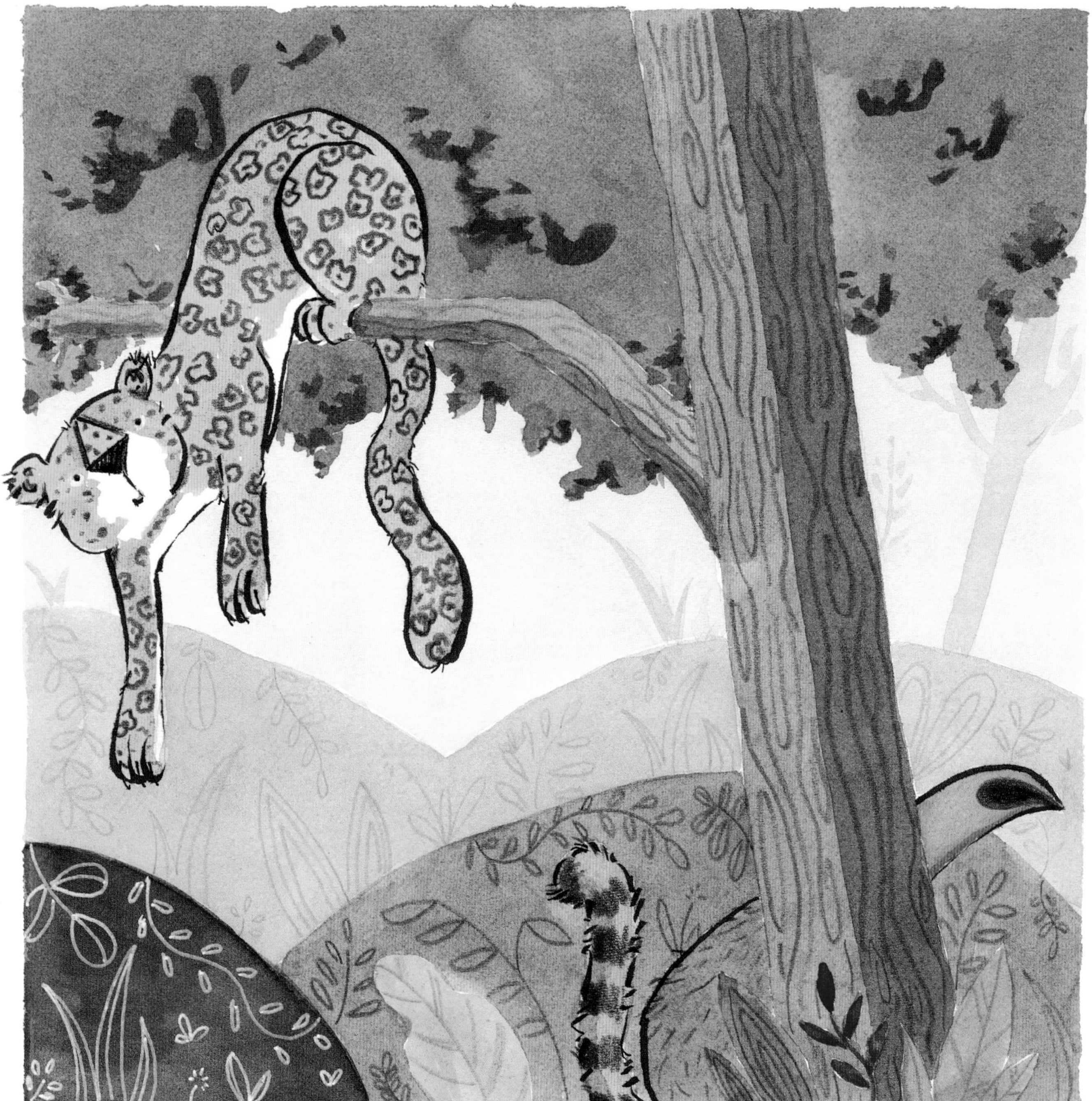

"But I heard its growly growl!"

"I saw its terrifying tail!"

"I spotted its menacing mane!"

"Nonsense," Jaguar said. "As a big cat myself, I can assure you this would be highly unusual. We're part of a big family, and we follow rules. I would be the first to know if ever a—"

"GRR, I'M

A LION!"

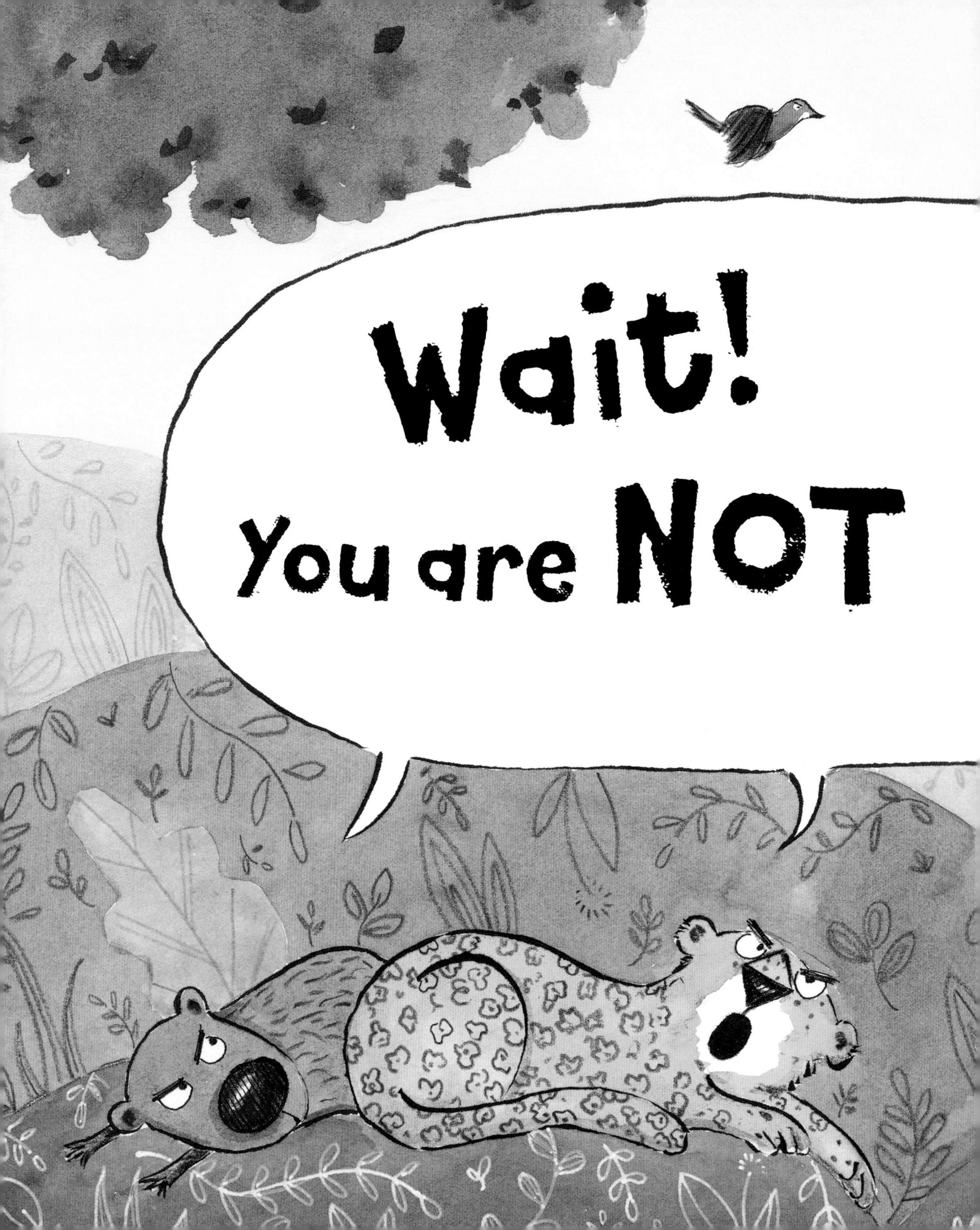
Wait! You are NOT

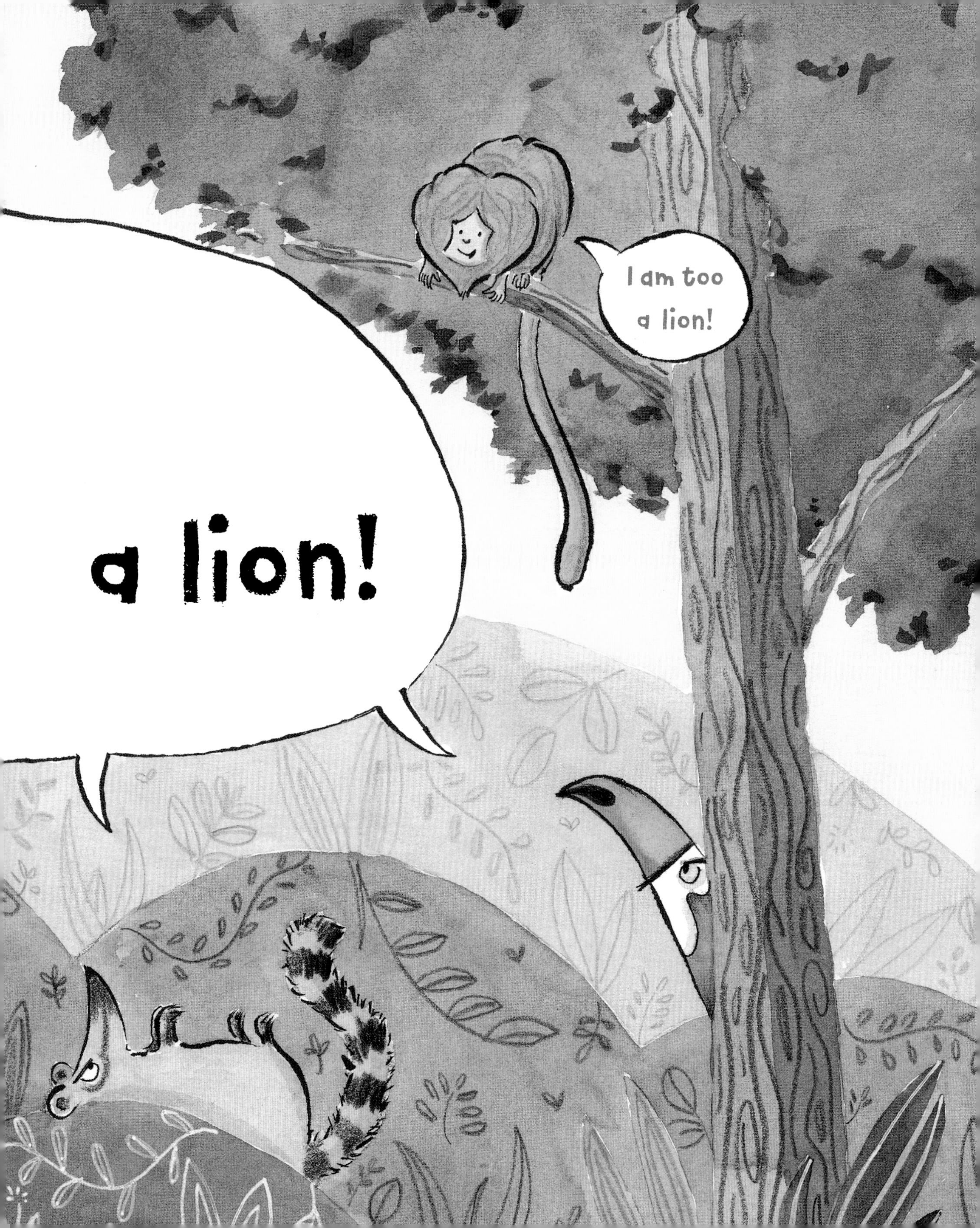
a lion!
I am too
a lion!

"See, I'm as strong as a lion!"

"I'm strong, too," said Capybara.

"Well, I have a long tail like a lion!"

"I have a long tail, too," said Coati.

"But I look like a lion!"

"Well, I look even more like one," said Jaguar.

"I can roar like a lion . . ."

"I can roar, too," said Toucan.

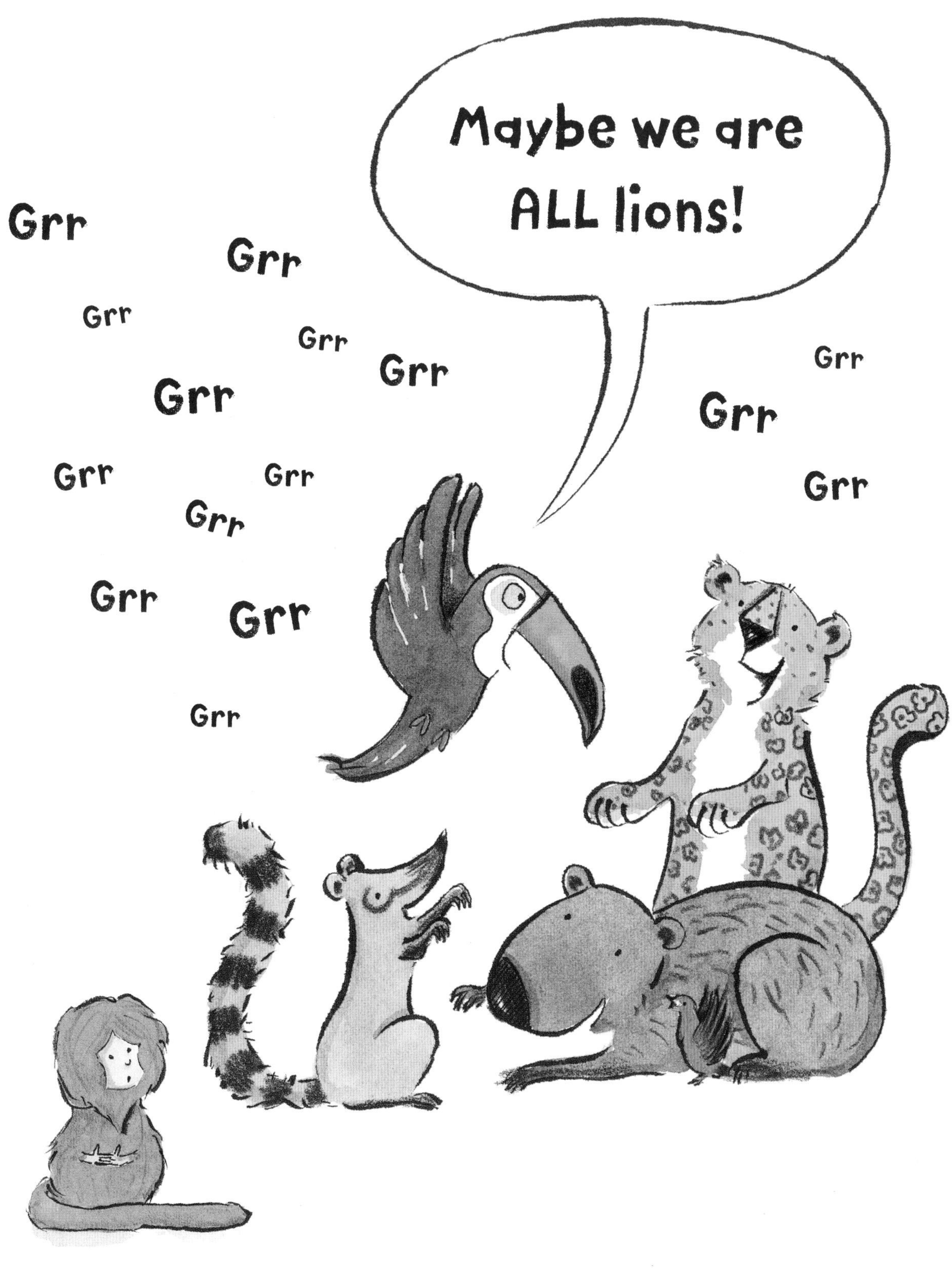
Maybe we are ALL lions!
Grr
Grr
Grr
Grr
Grr
Grr
Grr
Grr
Grr
Grr
Grr
Grr
Grr
Grr
Grr

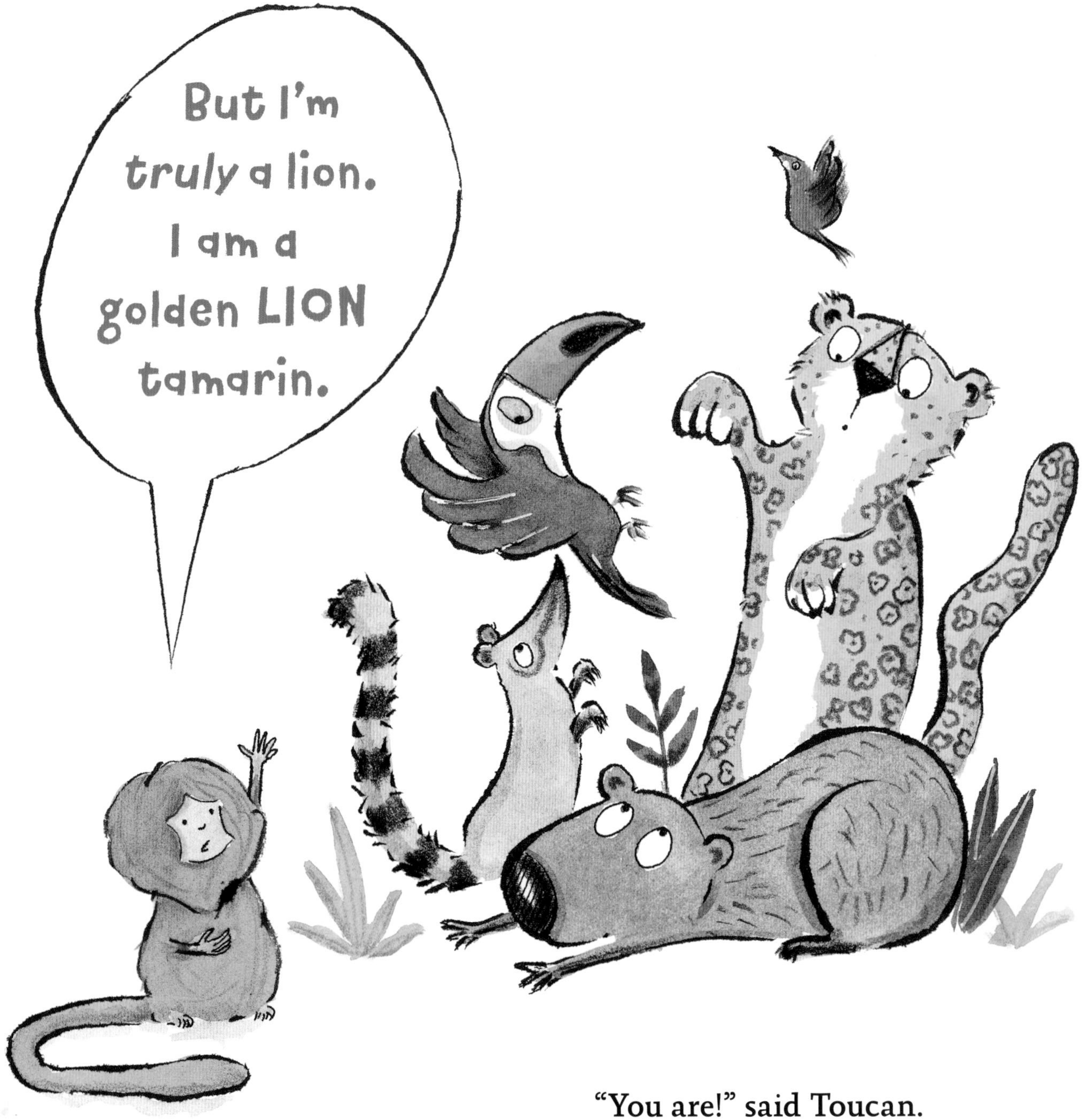
But I'm truly a lion. I am a golden LION tamarin.

"You are!" said Toucan.

"Then I was right all along."

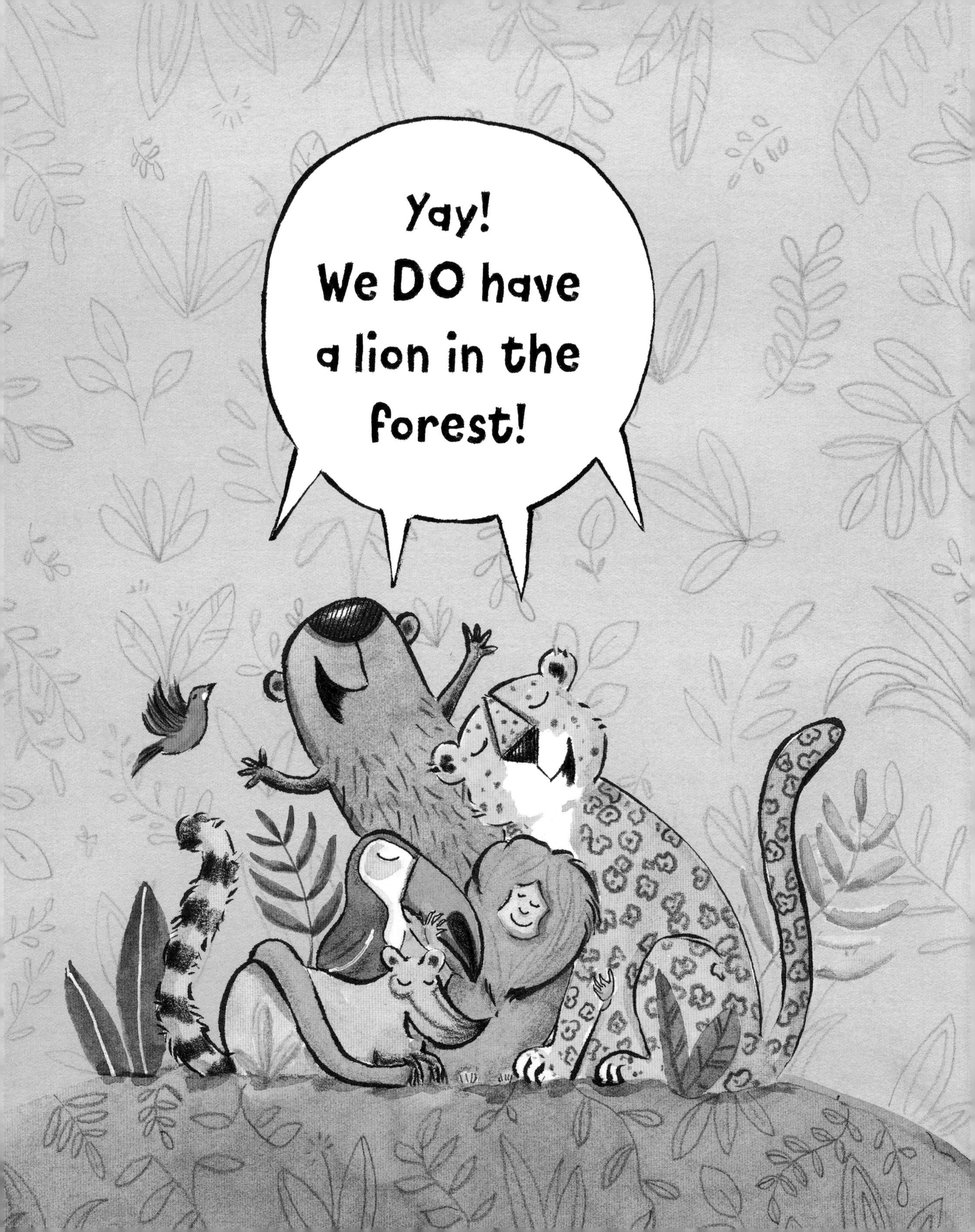
Yay! We DO have a lion in the forest!

The Animals of the Atlantic Forest of South America

TOUCANS live in the treetops of the forest. The toco toucan is the largest of the toucans and has a long orange beak that makes up almost a third of the bird's total length. They are a noisy bird, and they eat mostly fruit, though they also like small insects and tree frogs. **Fun fact: Toucans are not very good at flying and mostly travel by hopping from tree to tree.**

CAPYBARAS are the largest rodents in the world. They are also excellent swimmers, thanks to their slightly webbed feet. They are vegetarian and use their sharp teeth to graze on grass and water plants. **Fun fact: Capybaras also eat their own poop! They do so because it helps them digest their food better.**

COATIS are members of the raccoon family. They have a long, flexible snout that they use to search for food underneath rocks or between cracks in trees. Their diet consists of insects, fruit, and even small lizards and snakes. **Fun fact: Coatis walk with their long bushy tails held high, and use them for balance when climbing.**

BRAZILIAN TANAGERS are known for their striking plumage. The males of the species are bright red with black wings and tail. Their diet consists of mostly fruit, seeds, and insects. Their nests are built in the shape of a basket, and their eggs are blueish green with dark spots. **Fun fact: Brazilian tanagers are very adaptive and can be found even in city parks and public squares.**

JAGUARS are the biggest cats in the Americas. Their coats have dark spots that look like the outline of a rose with a small dark dot inside. They hunt day and night and possess excellent vision and a powerful bite. Their diet is varied and includes turtles, capybaras, and even caimans, a large alligator-like reptile. **Fun fact: Unlike most cats, jaguars love to swim.**

GOLDEN LION TAMARINS are part of the monkey family. Their reddish-gold fur and impressive lion-like mane make them easily recognizable. They live in small family groups, and their diet consists of flowers, fruit, and small insects. **Fun fact: Golden lion tamarin females usually give birth to twins.**

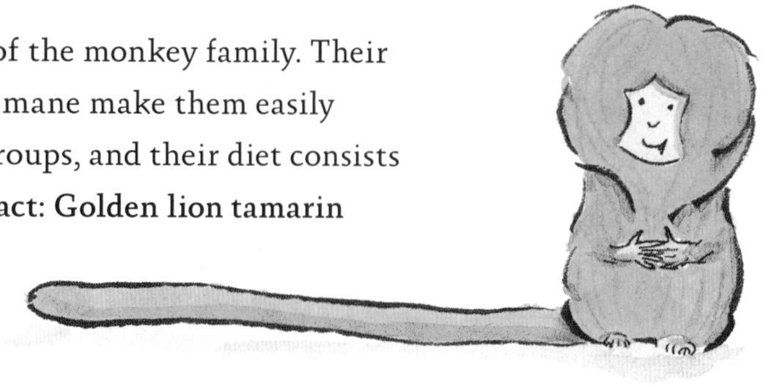

SAVING THE GOLDEN TAMARIN

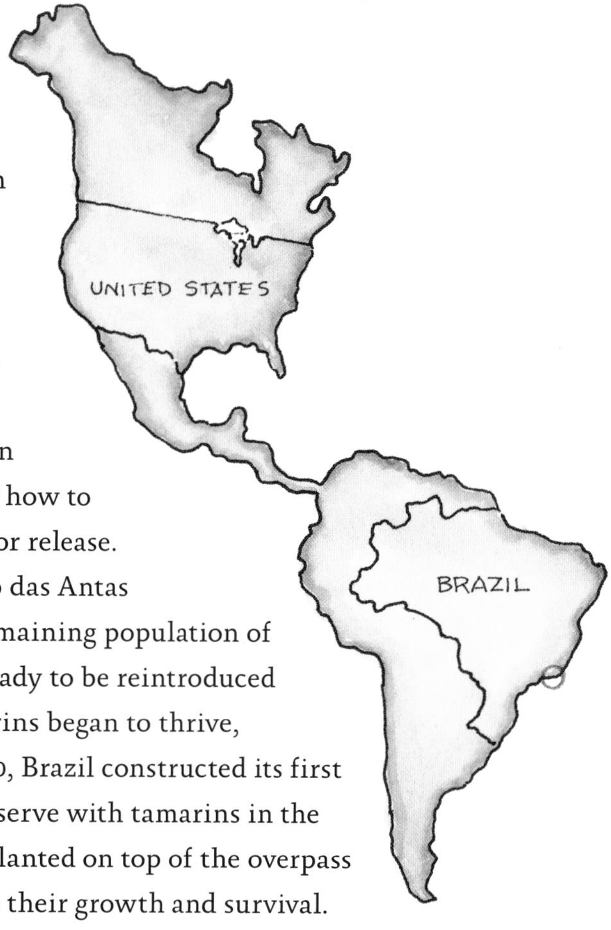
UNITED STATES
BRAZIL

Golden lion tamarins are an endangered species. By the early 1970s, there were fewer than 200 of them left in the wild, mostly due to the destruction of their natural habitat from timber harvesting, deforestation, and the rapid development of cities and roads. Fortunately, scientists, nonprofit organizations, and local communities joined forces to preserve the tropical forest and ensure the survival of its inhabitants, including the golden lion tamarin. Zoos joined the effort and began learning how to best raise tamarins in captivity and prepare them for release.

In 1974, the Brazilian government created Poço das Antas Biological Reserve (circle on map) to protect the remaining population of golden lion tamarins and to house new tamarins ready to be reintroduced into the wild. Captive and native golden lion tamarins began to thrive, increasing the need for more forested areas. In 2020, Brazil constructed its first wildlife overpass, connecting tamarins from the reserve with tamarins in the forest on the other side of a major highway. Trees planted on top of the overpass connect animals from both sides, helping to ensure their growth and survival.

In 2018, the Brazilian government proclaimed August 2 as National Golden Lion Tamarin Day.

For more information:

Markle, Sandra. *The Great Monkey Rescue: Saving the Golden Lion Tamarins*. Minneapolis: Millbrook Press, 2016.

Save the Golden Lion Tamarin (SGLT)
savetheliontamarin.org

Associação Mico-Leão Dourado (AMLD)
micoleao.org

"A Bridge for Tamarins." *The New York Times*: April 21, 2020.
nytimes.com/2020/04/21/science/tamarins-monkeys-brazil.html

Para os meus pais / For my parents
Bernadette & Carlos

Nancy Paulsen Books
An imprint of Penguin Random House LLC, New York

Nancy Paulsen Books and colophon are trademarks of Penguin Random House LLC.

Visit us online at penguinrandomhouse.com

Library of Congress Cataloging-in-Publication Data is available.

Manufactured in China
ISBN 9780399167010
1   3   5   7   9   10   8   6   4   2
TOPL

Design by Eileen Savage. Text set in Absara Pro and Canvas Text Sans.
The art was rendered with a Pentel brush pen, with Sennelier, Daniel Smith, and Winsor & Newton watercolors, and with Prismacolor pencils on Fabriano Artistico extra white 140 lb. hot pressed paper.